MICHAEL DAHL PRESENTS

PHOBIA

Don't Look Down

A TALE OF TERROR BY BRANDON TERRELL
ILLUSTRATED BY MARIANO EPELBAUM

STONE ARCH BOOKS
a capstone imprint

Michael Dahl Presents is published by Stone Arch Books,
A Capstone Imprint
1710 Roe Crest Drive
North Mankato, Minnesota 56003
www.mycapstone.com

Library of Congress Cataloging-in-Publication Data is available on
the Library of Congress website.

Summary: Simone Yang is afraid of heights. Like, REALLY afraid of
heights. Even flying alone on an airplane to visit her grandma for
the summer freaks her out. So when a creepy old broken-down
carnival comes to town, only the idea of impressing her new
friends is enough to get Simone to ride the Ferris wheel. But as the
ride creaks slowly toward the sky, can Simone keep her cool, or is
her worst fear about to come true?

ISBN: 978-1-4965-7912-6 (library hardcover)
ISBN: 978-1-4965-7914-0 (ebook PDF)

Printed and bound in the USA.
PA48

MICHAEL
DAHL
PRESENTS

Michael Dahl has written about werewolves, magicians, and superheroes. He loves funny books, scary books, and mysterious books. Every Michael Dahl Presents book is chosen by Michael himself and written by an author he loves. The books are about favorite subjects like monster aliens, haunted houses, farting pigs, or magical powers that go haywire. Read on!

ACROPHOBIA
(ak-ruh-FOH-bee-uh)

THE FEAR OF
HIGH PLACES

EVERYONE IS AFRAID OF SOMETHING.

I'm afraid of quite a number of things. But a **PHOBIA** is a very special fear. It is deep and strong and long lasting. It is hard to explain why people have phobias—they just do.

Riding in planes terrifies me. Flying through clouds, bumping into air currents, looking down on mountaintops! So I feel for Simone. If I was her I'd never go on that Ferris wheel.

Mr. Terrell, our author, hints that something weird is going on at the Forever Fun Carnival. It's not just the scary rides. There's more than one fear haunting these pages.

Michael Dahl

1

I squeezed my eyes shut and balled my hands into fists. For the hundredth time in the last five minutes, I prayed the plane wouldn't crash. Which was kind of ridiculous, considering I hadn't even boarded it yet.

"Simone? Are you sure you're all right?" my mom asked. She stood behind me as I looked out the airport's giant window at the plane I was about to take across the country.

I'd been excited about my summer trip to Gamma's for months. And it wasn't like I'd never flown on a plane before. I had, plenty. Only this time I was flying by myself. So I sucked it up, nodded, and said, "Perfect. Just sad to leave you guys." I turned to face my parents.

My mom, a worrier like me, was wringing her hands. My dad, much more relaxed, had his hands in his pockets.

"I mean, what will you guys do without me?" I asked.

Dad chuckled. "Have a clean house?" he said.

I rolled my eyes.

A voice came over the speaker. "Now boarding flight 815, nonstop from Chicago to Bangor, Maine."

"All right," I said. "Here I go."

Mom and Dad gave me a pair of extra-long hugs. "Be sure to listen to the flight attendants," Mom told me. "And Gamma will be at the gate waiting for you. OK?"

"OK."

I wheeled my purple carry-on luggage to the desk and handed the man my boarding pass. "Simone Yang," he said, reading the ticket. "Flying solo, I see."

I glanced at my waving parents. "Yep."

"Welcome aboard," the man said.

I followed the line of people down the metal corridor. With each step, my anxiety grew. I hated heights. No, check that, I hated the idea of *falling* from heights. And there's nothing quite like imagining yourself falling from heights when you're inside an enormous hunk of metal 30,000 feet in the sky.

I found my seat and stowed my luggage. There were three seats in my row. The window seat was taken by an older woman wearing so much jewelry she twinkled and chimed with every movement. I sat in the middle seat beside her.

I stuck in my earbuds and blasted my music. It drowned out the sound of the pilot speaking. It drowned out the sound of the safety video. It drowned out what to do in the event of a water landing.

I didn't want to think about a water landing.

I wanted to think about Gamma. And my friend Olive. And spending summer at the beach picking

shells and swimming. The plane taxied down the runway and began its powerful climb into the sky. My stomach dropped, my hands and neck began to sweat. I gripped the armrests tight and pictured my destination.

And it helped. Kind of.

When the plane leveled off, I peeled my hands from the armrests. The woman beside me had the shade up. A brilliant blue sky speckled with clouds filled the window.

There was a tap on my shoulder. I leapt up, startling the flight attendant who was trying to get my attention.

I plucked out my earbuds.

"Would you like something to drink?" the flight attendant asked.

"Oh," I said. "Um, no. I'm OK."

The flight attendant's drink cart rattled as she moved on down the aisle. I started to put my earbuds back in when the walking jewelry advertisement spoke. "Not a fan of flying, eh?" she asked.

"Nope," I said.

The airplane suddenly shook and dipped. My heart followed suit. I gasped and grabbed the woman's bracelet-heavy arm.

"It's OK, dear," the lady said reassuringly. "Very few planes actually crash because of turbulence."

I exhaled slowly and tried to calm my nerves. "Thanks," I said.

"No problem." The lady smiled. "Statistically, take-offs and landings are far more dangerous. That's when we're likely to crash."

Just like that, the anxiety was back.

With every shake, every rumble, every dip and turn, my heartbeat sped up and my fingers dug into the armrests harder.

They didn't let up until the wheels touched the tarmac in Bangor.

2

Olive was excited to see me when I reached the baggage claim. She rushed right up to me and hugged me. Olive lived next door to Gamma. We'd been friends since we were both wearing water wings on the beach, but since Olive lived here year-round and I didn't, we only saw each other in the summer. Olive had thick-rimmed glasses. Her shoulder-length hair was dusty blond this summer.

"So how was your flight?" Olive asked.

"It was fine," I lied.

"My word, Simone," Gamma said. "You are a bean sprout shooting to the sky. Just like your father." Gamma wrapped me in a comforting hug. She was short. At thirteen, I was just as tall as her. She wore her black hair pulled back in a ponytail.

"Love you too, Gamma," I said.

Olive took my hand and led the way back to Gamma's car, a baby-blue classic Volkswagen Bug. A speckling of rust rimmed each wheel. Otherwise the car was in great shape. She bought it after Papa died, about three years ago.

"Do you think those long legs will fit in my car?" Gamma asked, nudging me in the side and chuckling at her own joke.

When I climbed into the passenger seat I had to slide the seat back so my knees wouldn't touch the dashboard. I didn't say anything to Gamma about it, but I caught her looking over and smirking as we drove away from the airport.

The city was soon replaced by tall evergreens and a winding two-lane highway. It was amazing how quickly we traveled from the hum of activity to the peacefulness of the country.

As we went, Olive leaned forward between Gamma and my seats and talked about school being out for the summer. About her dog Charlie. About the friends at her new school. About pretty much everything that popped into her head.

Soon we were driving along the stretch of oceanside road that led into Sunset Cove. On our right, the deep blue of the Atlantic Ocean met the horizon. I rolled my window down. The cool ocean air, with its perfect salty smell, swirled around me and made my hair dance.

I loved that smell. I closed my eyes and breathed it in.

"There's the boardwalk!" Olive's shout broke my inner calm. "We're meeting my friends there later!"

I peeled one eye open. I had run across that boardwalk countless times. We had built sandcastles in its shadow for years. But something about the way Olive talked about it made me want to look.

What I saw made my breath catch in my throat.

Looming above the tree line was a gigantic, colorful Ferris Wheel. Its cars—red, blue, yellow and green—were not moving, but seemed to sway nonetheless.

"Whoa," I whispered.

"Cool, huh?" Olive said. "The carnival just came into town. Like, in the middle of the night! I had no idea it was going to take over the boardwalk."

As Gamma drove past the boardwalk, there was a break in the trees.

I spotted more attractions, including a metal roller coaster and a row of tents with games in them.

Next to the road, three men were hanging a banner on a broken billboard. Two stood on ladders while the other supervised from the ground. The banner read: Forever Fun Carnival.

As we drove past, the man on the ground turned. He wore dusty overalls and a bright red baseball cap pulled low on his head. His hard-edged face was lined with deep creases. He peered at the car. Peered at me.

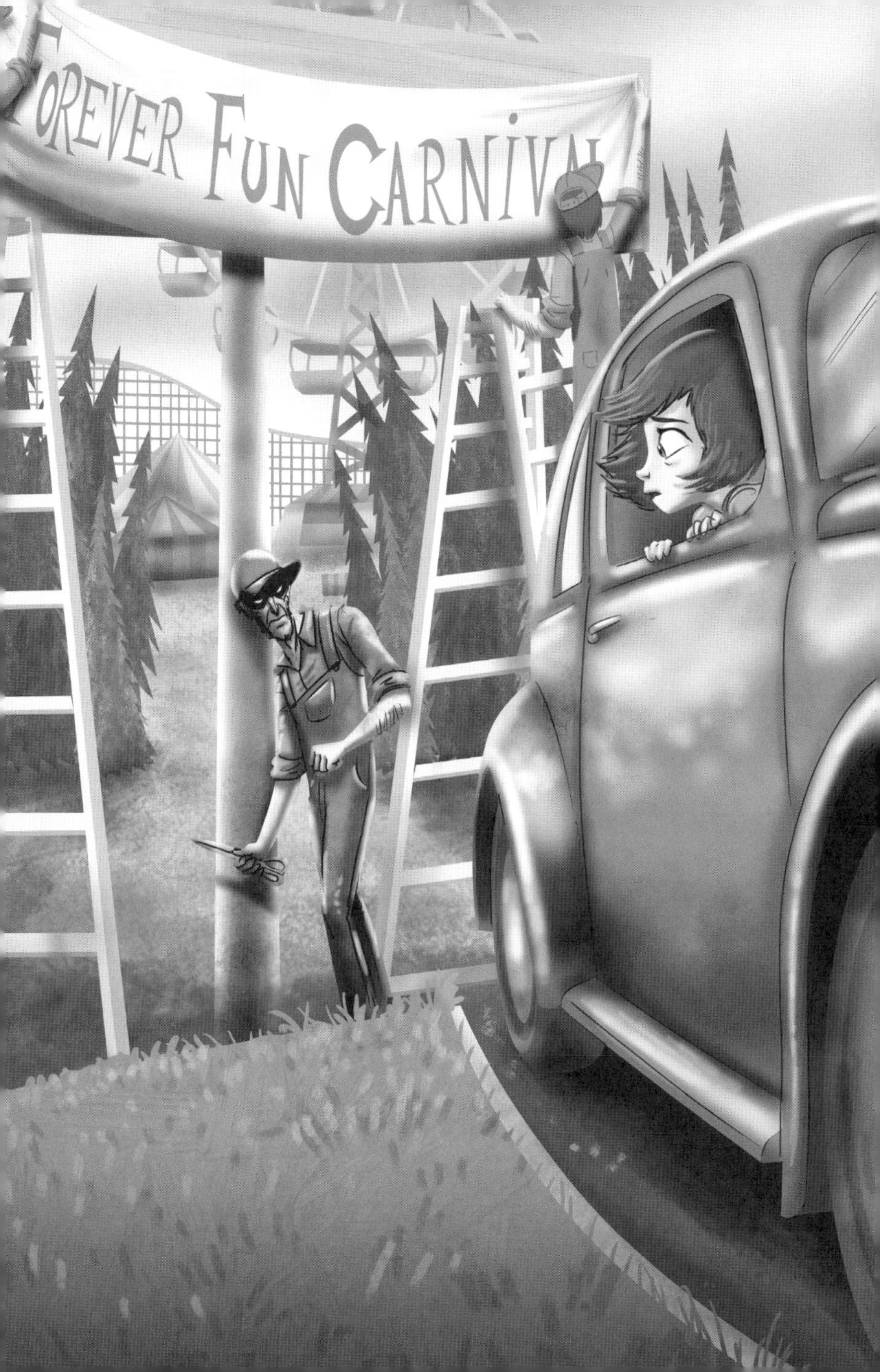
FOREVER FUN CARNIV

His gaze made the hair on the back of my neck stand. Suddenly, I was very cold. I rolled my window up.

"Everything OK?" Gamma asked.

I looked in the rearview mirror. The man was still watching us. He stared at the car until we rounded a corner and he disappeared.

"Yeah," I said. "Just . . . cold, I guess."

3

Gamma's house was a one-story cabin with wood siding and a huge screened-in porch. It sat at the top of a small hill in a cluster of other cabins, including the one owned by Olive's family. The hill led to a wide beach, where waves lapped at the sand and stones.

As the three of us got out of the car, a large, fluffy white dog raced out to greet us. It barked and jumped and wagged its tongue.

"Hey-ya, Chuck," I said, scratching Charlie behind an ear. "Miss me, boy?"

As if in response, Charlie woofed and licked my hand.

"Come on," Olive said to her dog. "Let's give Simone some time to settle in." Then she and Chuck raced off toward their house.

The inside of Gamma's cabin was cluttered. She had knickknacks and trinkets everywhere, much of it traced back to her Korean heritage.

I dropped my things in the bedroom in back. It was narrow, with a twin-size bed. On the dresser was a mirror covered in photos of me, Gamma, and Papa.

Gamma whipped up a meal of rice and fish, and we ate on the porch. I couldn't believe I got to spend the whole summer enjoying fresh-cooked meals, with the ocean accompanying our every bite.

"Be safe tonight," Gamma said as she cleaned our plates and I grabbed my bike helmet off a hook on the wall.

"We always are," I replied, hurrying out the door.

Olive was waiting. We hopped on our bikes and cruised down a path through the trees we'd created years ago. The sun cast long shadows and left pockets of light in the forest. It would be dark soon, and we'd have to be more cautious on our way home.

I pedaled hard, sailing off bumps in the path. Low-hanging branches whisked against our shoulders and helmets.

We broke from the last cluster of trees and into the light. The boardwalk lay straight ahead. Even though it wasn't yet dark, the carnival's lights glowed bright. The Ferris wheel slowly turned, its open cars filled with laughing kids and adults. Seeing it again made my stomach turn.

Olive must have seen the fear in my eyes. She skidded to a stop. "This'll be fun," she said. "I promise."

The moment I stepped onto the boardwalk's thick wooden planks, I could feel the rumbling roller coaster beneath my feet. Olive peered through the crowd.

"I don't see them," she said. Then she clasped a hand around my wrist. "But I do see something that you'll love!"

Tucked away, almost hidden from sight, was an old, glass fortune-teller machine. A statue of a man with a thin, twirling mustache smiled at us. In front of him was a glowing crystal ball. "Let ZOLTAR tell your FUTURE!" was painted on a nearby sign.

Olive dug out a pair of quarters. "Here," she said. "You go first."

As silly as these machines were, I did get a kick out of them. So I plucked the quarter from Olive's palm and plunked it into the Zoltar machine.

Zoltar's crystal ball began to flicker. The statue's head twisted back and forth. A tinny voice filtered out of the speaker. "Greetings," it said in a thick, unknown accent. "Zoltar knows all. Zoltar sees all. Let the light of my crystal ball guide you on your path."

A whiz and a click, and the flickering stopped. A slip of paper appeared in the slot alongside the speaker. I tore it off and read it.

You are right to be scared.

"Is this some kind of joke?" I asked no one in particular. Or maybe Zoltar. I didn't know. The

fortune in my hand was making it tremble. Like plane turbulence. Or a Ferris wheel in the sky.

"Oh, don't take it so seriously," Olive said "My turn!" She inserted her quarter and clapped as Zoltar did his song and dance, then ripped off her own fortune. I hoped my fears would go away when she read something strange like the silly fortune I'd just gotten.

"Watch over your friend," Olive read. "She will need your help."

"What?" I grabbed her wrist and pulled the fortune toward me so I could read it for myself.

Olive brushed me off. "Don't worry," she said with a chuckle. "This fortune is total nonsense. I always have your back."

"Olive!" came a loud voice from the crowd.

A group of kids was walking toward us. The girl in the lead waved to get our attention.

"Guys!" Olive dashed off in their direction. I gave the grinning, maniacal Zoltar one last glare and shoved my stupid fortune into my pocket.

4

Olive introduced me to her friends. There was Gwenda. She had curly brown hair that was this weird combination of perfect and "just out of bed." There were the twins, Steph and Keenan. Steph had long blond hair, and Keenan wore a buzzcut.

Then there was C.J. She stood out, both in her mannerisms and the fact that she actually stood away from the rest of us. C.J. had a fake-looking smile and flawless dark brown skin.

"Simone is spending the summer at her grandma's," Olive explained. "She just flew in a couple of hours ago."

"Hi guys," I said with a wave.

"Hi," Keenan and Steph said together. Gwenda waved.

C.J. said nothing, but offered a half-smile. Then she looked off toward the boardwalk's midway. "I'm bored. And I've got my eye on the ring toss."

Without another word, she headed toward the midway, expecting the rest of us to just follow along. And we did.

"What's her deal?" I asked Olive as we followed closely behind the group.

"She's nice once you get to know her," Olive said.

"Somehow I doubt that," I muttered.

I was frustrated that my time with Olive had become time with Olive and her friends.

We walked the midway, where C.J. bought a whole bunch of tickets. She spent way too many of them throwing softballs at milk jugs and tossing rings at old soda bottles while the others just watched and cheered her on. When she finally did ring a bottle and the carnival worker tried to give her a purple plush monkey as a prize, she wrinkled her nose and said, "Ew. No thanks."

Keenan snatched it up and tucked it under one arm. "Purple Monkey, you are mine," he said.

We hit a concession area, where I bought mini-donuts in a tiny paper bag. They were heavenly. Then Olive and I rode the Tilt-A-Whirl. We laughed as the ride spun, pressing us against each other. With each twirl, the carnival became a blur of lights and motion.

"That was amazing!" Olive and I cheered as the ride came to a stop.

Less amazing was the feeling I got as I stepped back onto the boardwalk. The wood beneath me felt like it was still moving, and I regretted the way I'd inhaled my mini-donuts.

"I need to sit down," I said, staggering toward a nearby bench.

I sat, head bowed, while my stomach calmed. Olive plopped down next to me and handed me a bottle of water. "You all right?" she asked.

"Yeah," I said. "Apparently flying across the country, eating a bag of mini-donuts, and violently spinning in circles is bad for the stomach. Who knew?"

I gave myself another moment, then breathed deep through my nose and stood.

"OK," I said. "What's next?"

"I kinda want to go on another ride," Gwenda suggested. "Maybe . . . the roller coaster?"

"Ooooh." Steph nodded. "Good call."

"Agreed," Keenan said.

The last thing me and my upset stomach needed was to get on the roller coaster. I shook my head. "I'll sit this one out," I said.

"Come on, Summer Girl," C.J. said with a coy smile. "It'll be fun. Right, Olive?"

Olive looked at me, then over at C.J., then back, like she was watching a tennis match. "I mean—" she started.

C.J. didn't let her finish. "I knew it!" she said, sliding her arm into Olive's and locking them together. "Olive's on board!" She began to strut away, my best friend in tow, leaving me behind.

And so, like I'd been doing all night, I followed them toward the rickety roller coaster.

5

As we neared the coaster, I heard my dad's voice in my head, quoting one of his favorite movies. "I've got a bad feeling about this . . ." I did have a bad feeling I couldn't shake, and it wasn't just the mini-donuts.

The roller coaster wasn't very tall, certainly not like an amusement park coaster and definitely not as tall as the Ferris wheel. But what it lacked in height it made up for in twists and turns.

As I looked around, it seemed as if the carnival crowd was thinning out. When we'd arrived, there had been people packed along the boardwalk. Even though it wasn't terribly late yet and the carnival wasn't set to close for a few more hours, it seemed less crowded now.

"Gwenda, you're up front with me!" C.J. chirped. She let go of Olive's arm and hurried over to snatch up Gwenda. Olive looked confused. Steph and Keenan were sure to pair off together, so that left Olive and me as a twosome. And if I wasn't going, then Olive would ride alone. C.J. was a lot smarter—and more conniving—than I first gave her credit for.

"Suppose you need someone to sit by," I said quietly to Olive.

"It's OK," she said. "I know you don't like heights."

"Or she's just trying to get attention," I heard C.J. mutter under her breath.

"No," I said, suddenly drawn by the urge to prove C.J. wrong. "I'll go with you."

I tried not to pay attention to the ride as we stood in line. I tried to ignore the groaning metal framework, and how the boardwalk shuddered every time a train of roller coaster cars passed. I tried not to imagine the ride crumpling or toppling over.

A ticket taker stood at the front of the line. He reminded me of the guy I saw earlier in the day. He had the same deep, chiseled creases etched across his face. He held out a hand and wiggled his bony fingers at me. "Ticket, please," he said with a grin.

The guy's dark, empty eyes and too-wide smile were creeping me out so much I almost turned back. Almost.

"Front car!" C.J. shouted. She and Gwenda climbed in.

Each car in the train held four people, two rows of two. Steph and Keenan also wanted the front car, so they climbed into a different one. This meant Olive and I were in the back, behind C.J. and Gwenda. Fine by me. I slid into the old metal seat, trying to hide how much my hands were shaking.

Olive lowered the bar across our laps until it clicked into place. It felt tight against my

midsection. I gripped the bar hard and made sure it was secure.

"You sure you're OK?" Olive whispered.

"Never better," I said through chattering teeth. I snuck a glance over my shoulder at the cars behind us.

The other trains, six of them, sat empty. We were the only ones on the ride. I was certain there had been people in line behind us. Hadn't there?

"Wait . . ." I started. " Where is . . . ?"

The car jerked forward before I could finish. I spun my head back around. C.J. had her arms up. The car slowly rounded a corner, then lurched forward as we began to climb.

I felt every click of the chain beneath us as the car rose. To my left, the ocean was inky black as far as the eye could see. The moon had retreated into the clouds, making the carnival the only beacon of light.

We kept climbing. I squeezed my eyes shut and held onto the bar even tighter.

It felt like an eternity. The clicking. The climbing. "How are we not at the top yet?" I whispered. The wind caught my words and swallowed them.

The coaster swayed back and forth. The metal track and support beams shuddered and moaned like an injured beast.

"Here we go!" C.J. screeched.

The climbing slowed, slowed, . . . slowed.

The car surged forward.

And we plummeted!

6

I screamed, but the wind slammed against my face and drowned it out. The sudden drop made my stomach claw its way into my throat and lodge itself there.

We hit the bottom of the track and twisted hard left. Olive and her friends cheered and hooted. With each turn, it felt like the car could topple off the track.

We rose and fell, rattled and clattered. Excitement cut through the fear, and for the briefest of moments, a smile flickered across my face. It was gone in an instant as the car's brakes engaged with a squeal and we slid back to the platform.

I'd done it. I'd survived the roller coaster.

I staggered out of the car on wobbly legs. The platform felt like it was swaying, like I was on the deck of a ship.

"That was so fun!" C.J. said, practically skipping down the platform and back onto the boardwalk with Gwenda. Keenan proudly held up the stuffed animal and proclaimed, "Purple Monkey gives it two opposable thumbs up!"

"Wait up!" Olive brushed past me to catch up with them.

Behind me, the coaster clattered as another set of riders began to climb the first rise. As I looked closer, though, I noticed there weren't any riders. The cars were empty. It reached the top, shot down, loudly clattered past me and curved away. The structure shuddered as they vanished.

Tink . . . tink . . . tink . . .

Something fell from above, hitting the coaster's metal support beams and landing on the boardwalk. It was hard to see through the thick shadows under the coaster.

But I saw it. And when I realized what it was, my stomach sank like it was back on the coaster.

Had a piece of the roller coaster really just fallen off? And was I the only person who saw it?

A small plastic fence had been set up around the ride for safety, but I wanted to confirm my suspicions. So I stepped closer.

It was a shiny metal screw.

The shadows under the coaster moved, startling me. A figure emerged, a man in dirty overalls and a baseball cap.

The man from the highway.

Without a word, he bent down, picked up the fallen screw, and pocketed it. I tried to retreat, but my feet wouldn't move. The man locked eyes with me. The shivers that had coursed through me the first time I'd seen him returned stronger than before.

He vanished back into the shadows.

I was done with this place. I wanted to go back to Gamma's.

"Olive!?" I shouted as I stumbled away from the roller coaster. I ran along the boardwalk, looking for my friend. "Olive!"

"Simone?!" Olive cried back. She and the others had stopped up ahead. Maybe to wait for me, but probably not. C.J. stood with her arms crossed while the others tossed Purple Monkey around. None of them seemed to notice that the crowd was basically gone now.

"What's up?" Olive asked as I reached her.

"I'm leaving," I said.

"What?"

"I'm going back to Gamma's," I said. "This place . . ." It felt weird to say it out loud. "This place has been creeping me out since the moment we got here."

Olive spoke in a low voice. "Is this about my friends?" She cast a glance over her shoulder.

"What?" I replied. "No."

"Then stay," Olive said. "You liked the roller coaster, right?"

Until a piece of it fell off! I thought.

"I just . . . wanna go home," I said. "I want to hang out on the beach. And read books. And swim. And collect shells and rocks. With you."

"So it *is* about my friends." Olive put her hands on her hips and glared at me.

I shook my head and said, "Whatever." Then I stalked away.

"Bye, Summer Girl!" C.J. sang.

I didn't turn around. I walked through the carnival, now practically empty, until I reached the exit.

A twinkle of light caught the corner of my eye. I turned to see Zoltar smiling at me. Angrily, I stomped over to the machine and dug in my pocket. I still had a quarter left.

I don't know why I wanted another fortune. Maybe to prove the goofy thing was random, that it had a bunch of different sayings in it and that my first fortune was a fluke.

I plunked a coin into the slot and let Zoltar glow and flicker and talk in its cheesy voice. I wasn't amused. All I wanted was the slip of paper at the end.

When it came, I ripped it off and immediately read it. "You are right to be scared," I whispered.

I'd gotten the exact same fortune.

7

"Arrgh!" I ripped up the fortune, dropped it on the boardwalk, and stomped on it for good measure. Zoltar smiled back at me, a glint of menace in his painted eyes.

"What is going on with this place?" I didn't say it loud, but my voice seemed to carry. I glanced around the boardwalk, but there weren't any families running around. No couples holding hands and carrying oversized stuffed animals like Purple Monkey. Nobody but me.

Where had everyone gone?

"Hello?" I called out.

No one answered. But there was movement ahead, near the start of the midway. A man appeared from behind one of the tents, shuffling out to the middle of the boardwalk. Another carnival worker.

And he looked just like the man in the overalls.

I quickly ran off the boardwalk and toward the path where Olive and I had left our bikes. Sand from the beach kicked up behind me. It slipped inside my shoes, grinding between my toes. I didn't care.

It wasn't until I reached the bikes, propped against a tree at the edge of the wooded path, that I noticed how very dark it was. The moon was still hidden in the clouds, snuffing out its usual blue glow. It was like the carnival was sapping the light out of everything around it.

I grabbed the handlebars and turned my bike toward the path in the woods. At least, where I thought the path in the woods was. All I could see was blackness.

And it was quiet. So very quiet.

When I noticed the absolute silence around me, I couldn't stop shivering. The carnival was not far away. I should've still been able to hear its creepy music or hear the clattering roller coaster cars. But there was nothing. Not even the ocean waves made noise.

The black woods loomed before me.

Quiet.

Empty.

There was no way I could ride back to Gamma's house in the dark by myself.

So I did what I should have done right away. I dug out my phone and called Gamma for a ride.

She picked up on the third ring. "Hi, sweetheart. Is everything OK?" she asked. She sounded like I'd woken her up. "Are you having a fun time with Olive and her friends?"

"No, Gamma," I said. "I need a ride home." I had begun to cry, and used the bottom of my T-shirt to wipe my eyes and nose.

There was a crackle on the phone. A long pause.

Then: "Simone?"

Gamma sounded confused. "Simone, are you there, hon?"

"Gamma?" I said, louder. "Gamma. Yes. It's me. I'm here. I want to come home." My voice shook.

Another long pause. More crackling.

"Well, this goofy thing just isn't working," Gamma said, more to herself than to me. "Simone, if that's you, I can't hear a darn thing. Try calling me—"

Crackle. And then she was gone.

The town of Sunset Cove wasn't exactly in the middle of nowhere. Reception and dropped calls shouldn't have been a problem. Frustrated, I began to dial Gamma's number again.

As I punched 'Send,' my phone winked out.

Black screen.

Dead.

8

"What?" I punched at the phone screen and pressed the power button. It had to be a mistake. I should have had enough charge to make it through the night.

But then I thought about the plane ride. I'd blasted music for two-plus hours in an attempt not to think about crashing. Maybe my phone's battery was sapped.

I looked around at the darkness and thought about riding my bike back alone. *This would be so much better with Olive,* I thought.

Maybe I could convince Olive to come back with

me. Or at least convince her to let me use her phone to call Gamma. Gamma was probably worried that I hadn't immediately called back.

So I strode back into the Forever Fun Carnival, past the Zoltar machine, and toward the roller coaster. The boardwalk was nearly empty now. The only sounds came from the midway, from the clattering of empty rides and the tinkling, eerie music.

Olive and her friends weren't hard to spot. They were walking together down the middle of the boardwalk.

C.J. was, of course, the first one to see me. "She's back!" She threw her arms up like she wanted to hug me. "What a fun surprise, Summer Girl."

"Stop calling me that," I said. I turned to Olive. "Can I use your phone? I need to call Gamma and my phone is dead."

"Gamma?" Gwenda repeated with a snicker. Great, even the rest of Olive's crew was starting to make fun of me.

Olive took my arm and pulled me aside.

"Simone, you're pale and sweating," she said. "What's going on?"

"Don't you see?" I tried to whisper, to keep myself calm. But it was hard. The words pushed their way out, louder than I'd intended. "This carnival . . . it's weird. The people working here all look the same. The rides are falling apart. This whole place is deserted and you don't even seem to notice."

Olive's face scrunched up in confusion. "What are you talking about?"

"We're the only ones here," I said.

"No," Olive said, shaking her head and sliding an arm around my shoulder. "We're not."

"Wait . . . what?" I looked around.

Olive was right. The crowd hadn't disappeared at all. There were people everywhere. I turned in a full circle, taking in the carnival with awed disbelief. "But—" I started. "Just a second ago . . ."

"Look," Olive said calmly, "you've had a long day. I get it. You're tired and jet-lagged and maybe those mini-donuts really did a number on you. But there's nothing unusual about this place. Nothing to be scared of."

I pulled the fortune out of my pocket. "What about this, though?" I asked. "'You're right to be scared.'"

Olive did the same—took her fortune out and held it next to mine. "'Watch over your friend,'" she said. "So here I am. Watching over you. OK?"

I took a deep breath and looked out again at the people of Sunset Cove enjoying the carnival. I heard screams of delight from the roller coaster and Tilt-A-Whirl. The delicious scent of corndogs drifted through the sea breeze. Kids were walking everywhere, holding ice cream cones that dripped down to their hands.

I crumpled up Zoltar's fortune and dropped it onto the boardwalk. It slipped between a thin gap in two planks of wood and vanished from sight. A wave of relief washed over me.

I was fine.

"One more ride and we'll head back home together," Olive said. "Promise."

"Hey, you two!" C.J. called out. She and the others were watching us. "We're heading to the Ferris wheel. You coming or what?"

I looked over at Olive, whose arm was still draped over my shoulder.

"Sure," I blurted out before I could stop myself.

9

My fear of the Forever Fun Carnival had subsided. But I was still deathly afraid of heights. So why I'd agreed to join the group on the Ferris wheel made little sense. Maybe it was Olive's confidence and support. Or maybe it was because I'd already bested the roller coaster.

Whatever it was, here we stood, in line for the Ferris wheel. Just a normal group of kids (and one stuffed purple monkey), enjoying a night at the carnival.

"How are you now?" Olive whispered as we neared the front of the line. The young man taking tickets looked nothing like the creepy old dude from the highway. Only his red ball cap was the same.

"Great," I answered. And it was mostly the truth.

The car waiting at the bottom of the Ferris wheel was purple. Keenan insisted it was a sign he and Steph should go first.

"Tickets, please," the man said to Steph and Keenan. They each plunked a pair of red tickets in his hand and took their spot.

"See you on the other side," Steph said. Keenan waved Purple Monkey's hand and they began to climb toward the night sky.

C.J. and Gwenda went next, passing off tickets and climbing into a yellow car.

I had two tickets in my hand. Nervously, I passed them to the man. "Climb aboard," he said with a smile. A red car had slowed to a stop at the bottom. I got in and waited for Olive.

But Olive was still talking to the ticket man. She searched her pockets, concerned. "I know I had more than one," I heard her say.

"You need two tickets to ride," the man replied.

The bar above slammed down, startling me. "Olive?!" I shouted.

Olive looked up at me. "What's going on?" she asked.

The ticket man smiled wide. Creases formed across his face, and he suddenly didn't look as young. "The ride must go on," he said to me. "Your friend will catch the next car."

My heart thundered against my ribcage. I tried to pull the bar up, to get out of the car and back to Olive. It was too late, though.

With a long creak, the Ferris wheel began to move again. I lifted off the ground, away from the boardwalk, away from Olive.

"Simone!" Olive cried.

"Olive!" I shouted back. I bent over and tried to look down and find her. All I could see, though, was the carnival getting smaller and smaller as I kept rising.

"What's going on down there, Summer Girl?"

C.J. asked from above. She and Gwenda laughed. Their car creaked back and forth over my head, like they were rocking it. Higher, out of my sight, Keenan made monkey noises while his sister cheered him on.

I held on tight to the bar. My knuckles were bone-white. The Ferris wheel did not stop for more riders. I crept higher and higher. In each direction, the blackened waves of the Atlantic Ocean were all I could see.

Cold sweat ran down my forehead and into my eyes, making them sting.

So I squeezed them shut.

"Just make it one time around," I whispered to myself. "Get back to the bottom and Olive will be there waiting for you."

Time stretched as I kept rising. I couldn't hear C.J. and Gwenda laughing anymore. I couldn't hear their car swinging. Keenan's monkey howls were gone as well. It was just me and the groaning, straining sound of the Ferris wheel.

Even with my eyes closed, I knew when I'd

reached the top. Instead of rising, my car began moving backward. In just a second, I'd start my descent toward the boardwalk again and this tortuous ride would be over.

That was when the Ferris wheel shuddered to a stop.

10

I hung suspended in the air, high above the boardwalk. I was too terrified to look down. The wind snuck up on me. It howled and made my hair dance. I could feel each beat of my heart in my ears. Each breath was a thin rasp.

Forever. I was going to be here . . . forever.

Alone.

I don't know how long I sat swaying, eyes closed, praying I'd see Gamma and Olive and my parents again. But then the ride trembled and my car began to move again.

"Oh, thank goodness," I whispered. I peeled one hand from the bar and used it to wipe the tears from my eyes. I was getting lower and lower. And the closer I got to the ground, the safer I felt.

I'd made it.

"Olive?" I shouted when I'd nearly reached the bottom. "I'm here! And I wanna get off this stupid thing!"

When I'd made it down, when I could see the boardwalk beneath me, I tried to lift the bar. "Let me off!" I said to the young man operating the ride.

Only he wasn't there anymore. Standing at the base of the Ferris wheel was the old man from the highway. Red ball cap. Overalls. Wide smile that looked eerily like Zoltar's.

"What?" The panic was back. "No," I whispered, looking beyond the man, at the boardwalk. "NOOO!!"

The carnival was gone. No rides. No concessions. No crowds of people. No C.J. or Gwenda or Keenan or Steph.

And no Olive.

I was alone. It was just me and the creepy old man and the Ferris wheel.

From the shadows, more figures emerged. More carnival workers. And they all looked the same, wearing the same crazed smile as the old man. Identical creased faces and red caps and overalls.

They all stared at me.

"Let me off!" I shouted again. I tried harder to free myself from the Ferris wheel. But the car didn't stop. Soon I was climbing toward the sky again.

I looked at the cars around me. They were all empty. The group of carnival workers, with their identical faces and expressions, craned their necks to watch as I rose into the black night again.

Something fluttered through the air in front of me. It struck me on the chest, then fell to my lap. I let go of the bar with one hand and grabbed it.

It was a slip of paper. A fortune. My fortune. Only now, the words had changed.

WE WARNED YOU, it read.

"Help!" I shouted at the top of my lungs as I climbed higher . . . higher . . .

Higher.

GLOSSARY

conniving (cuh-NYE-ving)—to be scheming or plotting something in secret

eerie (EER-ee)—strange and frightening

etch (ECH)—engrave or carve into something

glint (GLINT)—to sparkle or flash

heritage (HER-i-tij)—traditions and beliefs that a country or society considers an important part of its history

identical (eye-DEN-ti-kuhl)—exactly the same

loom (LOOM)—to appear suddenly or in a scary manner

lurch (LURCH)—to move in a sudden and uneven way

mannerism (MAH-nuh-ri-zum)—a certain behavior showing how someone acts

plummet (pluh-met)—to drop sharply

reception (ri-SEP-shuhn)—the way in which someone or something is received

speckling (SPEK-ling)—a tiny piece, spot or mark

tortuous (TAWR-choo-uhss)—full of twists and turns

trinket (TRING-kit)—a small, cheap object

turbulence (TUR-byoo-luns)—swirling winds that create strong air resistance; turbulence can quickly slow down an aircraft

FACE YOUR FEAR!

Now that you've read the story, it's no longer only inside this book. It's also in your brain. Can your brain help you answer the prompts below?

1. Simone isn't happy about spending time with Olive's friends. Why do you think Simone is hurt by hanging out with Olive's new friends?

2. Simone describes all the carnival workers as having identical faces. Why do you think that is?

3. Olive was told by the fortune-teller machine to watch over Simone. Write about what you would do if a fortune-teller machine told you to watch over your best friend.

4. Simone feels worried about her flight from Chicago, Illinois, to Bangor, Maine. Write down all the things Simone experiences on her plane trip that make her feel anxious.

5. Right before Simone gets onto the Ferris wheel, Olive discovers she can't get on. Write down what you think would have happened if Olive went on the ride. Would it have gone the same way?

FEAR FACTORS

acrophobia (ak-ruh-FOH-bee-uh)—the fear of high places

Acrophobia is also the fear of falling from those high places. It's fitting that Simone is the main character in our story, because twice as many women as men have this phobia.

Many people grow out of a phobia. But not with acrophobia. As we age, our sense of balance grows gradually weaker. Experts believe that is why so many people develop acrophobia later in life. A weak sense of balance can give you a fear of falling, so high places often become a source of fear, and something to avoid.

The most common nightmare of humans all across the world is the dream of falling.

Most scientists believe that you are born with acrophobia. But a few think that a fear of heights comes from a "trigger event" when you were younger. Perhaps you fell while playing. Or perhaps you saw a movie or TV show where something bad happened to people who were way up high.

Animals may also have acrophobia. The fear of heights in a puppy or kitten or little chick helps protect them by keeping them away from dangerously high places.

This phobia is connected to several other types: basophobia, the fear of falling, and batophobia, the fear of getting too close to a tall building.

ABOUT THE AUTHOR

Brandon Terrell has been a lifelong fan of all things spooky, scary, and downright creepy. He is the author of numerous children's books including several volumes in Capstone's Spine Shivers and Snoops, Inc. series. When not hunched over his laptop writing, Brandon enjoys watching movies (horror movies, especially!), reading, baseball, and spending time with his wife and two children in Minnesota.

ABOUT THE ILLUSTRATOR

Mariano Epelbaum is a character designer, illustrator, and

traditional 2D animator. He has been working as a professional artist since 1996, and enjoys trying different art styles and techniques. Throughout his career Mariano has created characters and designs for a wide range of films, TV series, commercials, and publications in his native country of Argentina. In addition to Michael Dahl Presents: Phobia, Mariano has also contributed to the Fairy Tale Mix-ups, You Choose: Fractured Fairy Tales, and Snoops, Inc. series for Capstone.

MICHAEL
DAHL
PRESENTS

The Lost Lenore

The Gulliver Giant

The Minotaur Maze

The Final Frankenstein

only from capstone